I Forgot to Say
I Love You

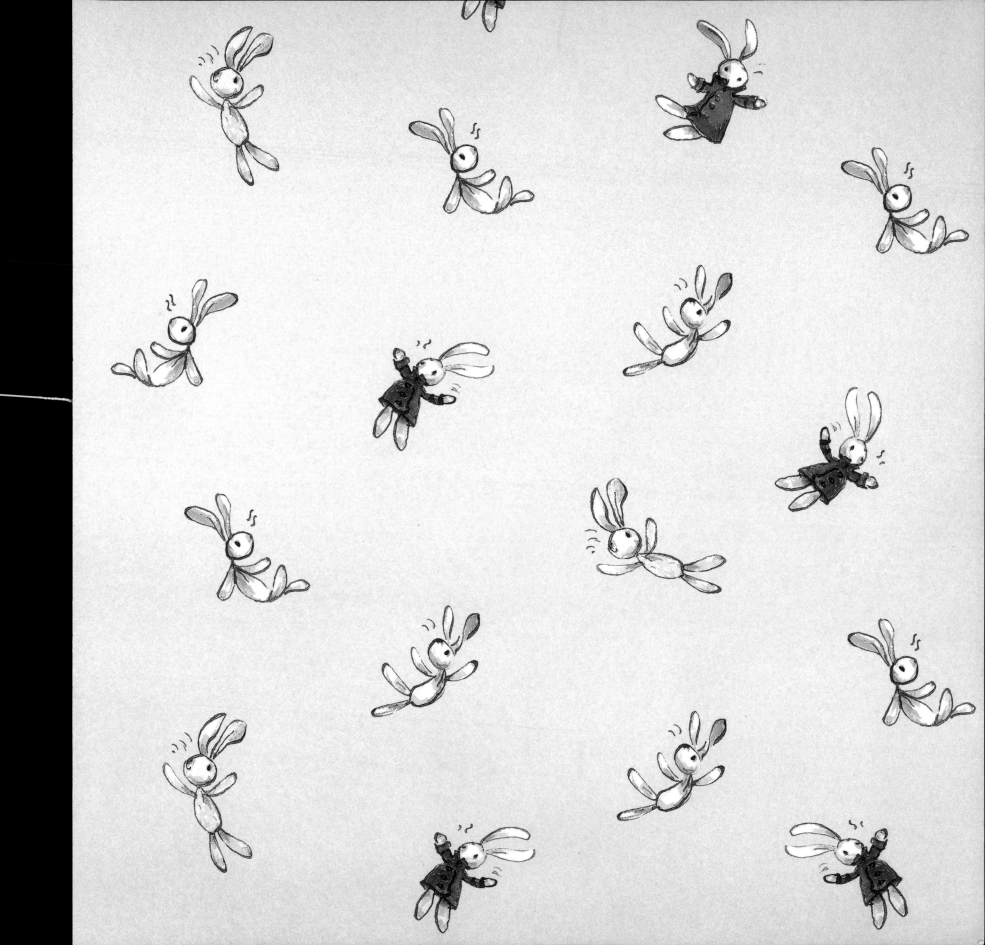

For Imogen, Morwenna and Finn – M.M.

For Jack and Kerenza – A.C.

First published 2003 by Macmillan Children's Books
This edition published 2004 by Macmillan Children's Books
a division of Macmillan Publishers Limited
20 New Wharf Road, London N1 9RR
Basingstoke and Oxford
Associated companies throughout the world
www.panmacmillan.com

ISBN 978-0-333-97234-2

Text copyright © Miriam Moss 2003
Illustration copyright © Anna Currey 2003
Moral rights asserted.

7 9 8

A CIP catalogue record for this book is available from the British Library.

Printed in China

I Forgot to Say
I Love You

MIRIAM MOSS

Illustrated by ANNA CURREY

MACMILLAN CHILDREN'S BOOKS

When Billy woke up, Rabbit was
hiding down the side of his bed.
"Don't think I can't see you there, Rabbit,"
said Billy, tugging at Rabbit's paw.

"Time for breakfast,"
Mum called from downstairs.
"In a minute," shouted Billy.
"Rabbit's being naughty."

"Come and wash your
sticky paws,"
called Mum.

"In a minute," said Billy.
"Rabbit won't eat her egg.
Hurry up, Rabbit!"

Billy and Rabbit went upstairs to get dressed.

Mum popped her head round the door.

"Get dressed, Billy," she said.

"In a minute," said Billy.

"I think Rabbit's got a

tummy ache."

"Come and brush your teeth, Billy," Mum called.

"In a minute," said Billy.

"Rabbit's buttons are all wrong."

"Get ready first, Billy, then play with Rabbit,"

said Mum.

"Dressed at last!" said Mum. "But where did I put your boots?"

"They're on my feet," laughed Billy.

"Oh good," smiled Mum. "Here's your coat. Come on.
We really must go or we'll be late!"

But Billy dashed upstairs.
"Just a minute!" he called.
"Rabbit hasn't said goodbye to the others."

On the way to nursery, Billy balanced Rabbit
and his lunch box on his head.
"Be careful," said Mum.
"I am," said Billy, "except Rabbit won't sit still."

Suddenly, Billy's lunch box hit the ground and burst open.

"Oh Billy!" said Mum, crossly.
"Now we really will be late."

"Give Rabbit to me and let's get a move on."

But they were very late and had to run the rest
of the way to nursery.

"Ah, there you are," said Mrs Brown.
"We wondered where you were."
"Sorry," panted Mum. "I must dash, I'm late
for work already. Bye Billy."
And she hurried away.

Billy hung his coat up.

"Is something the matter, Billy?" asked Mrs Brown.

"Mum didn't say *I love you*," said Billy.

"She always says *I love you*."

"She was in a bit of a hurry,"
said Mrs Brown.
"Have you left Rabbit by your peg?
She'll make you feel better."

They looked in Billy's pockets and even in his lunch box.

But Rabbit was nowhere to be found.

"You must have left her at home," said Mrs Brown.

"But I didn't," said Billy, starting to cry. "I dropped my lunch box and we had to run and now Rabbit's lost and I want my mum."

Suddenly the door flew open.

It was Mum!

"Oh Billy, I'm so sorry," she cried.
"I forgot to give Rabbit back to you, and I forgot
something else, too . . ."

" . . . I forgot to say I love you."

Billy climbed on to Mum's lap and gently she dried his tears.

"I love you, too," said Billy.
And they gave each other a
big, big hug.

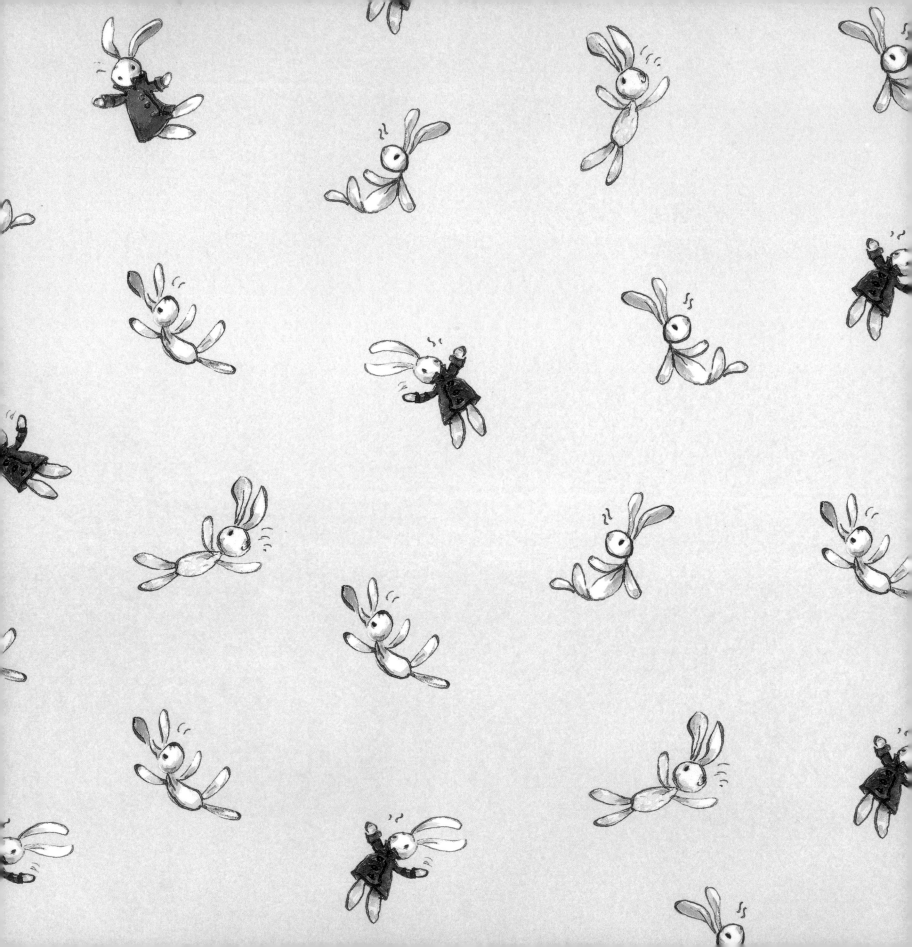

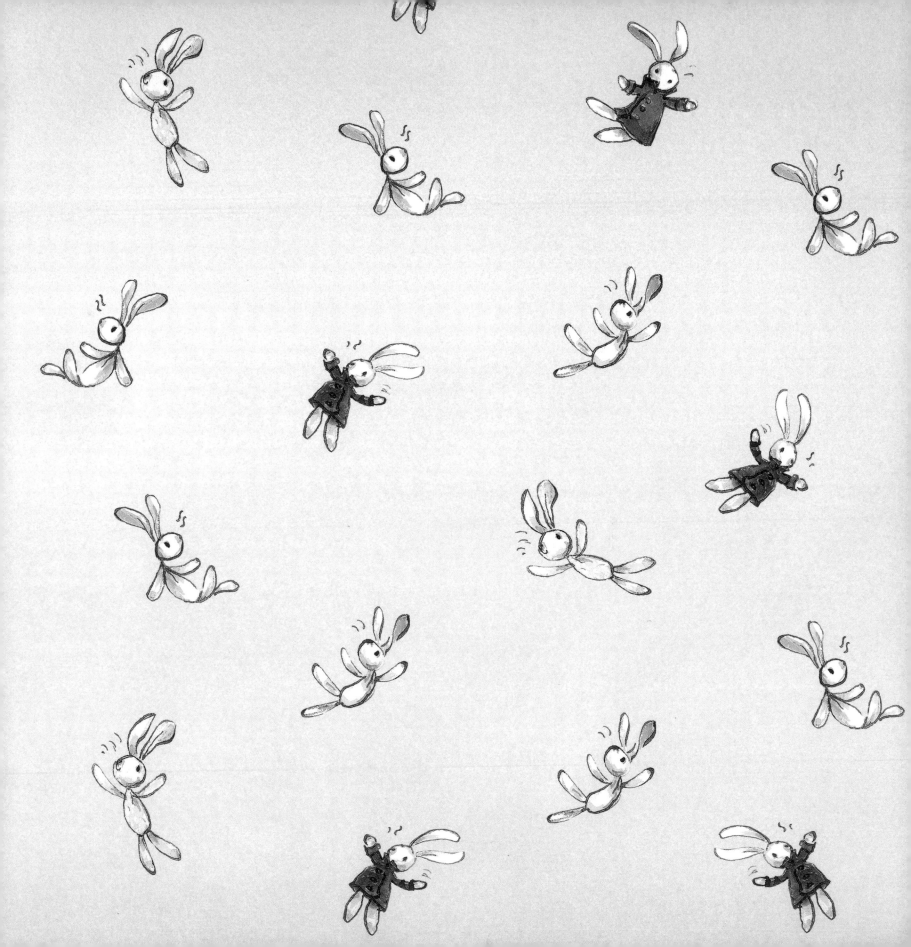